P9-APF-573

HORRID
HENRY
TRICKS THE
TOOTH FAIRY

Meet HORRID HENRY
the laugh-out-loud
worldwide sensation!

* Over 15 million copies sold in 27 countries and counting

* # 1 chapter book series in the UK

* Francesca Simon is the only American author to ever win the Galaxy British Book Awards Children's Book of the year (past winners include J.K. Rowling, Philip Pullman, and Eoin Colfer).

"Horrid Henry is a fabulous antihero…**a modern comic classic.**" —*Guardian*

"**Wonderfully appealing to girls and boys alike**, a precious rarity at this age." —Judith Woods, *Times*

···

"The best children's comic writer." —Amanda Craig, Times

···

"**I love the Horrid Henry books by Francesca Simon.** They have lots of funny bits in. And Henry always gets into trouble!" —Mia, age 6, *BBC Learning Is Fun*

"My two boys love this book, and **I have actually had tears running down my face and had to stop reading because of laughing so hard**." —T. Franklin, Parent

"**It's easy to see why Horrid Henry is the bestselling character for five- to eight-year-olds.**" —*Liverpool Echo*

"Francesca Simon's truly horrific little boy is **a monstrously enjoyable creation**. Parents love them because Henry makes their own little darlings seem like angels." —*Guardian Children's Books Supplement*

"I have tried out the Horrid Henry books with groups of children as a parent, as a babysitter, and as a teacher. **Children love to either hear them read aloud or to read them themselves**." —Danielle Hall, Teacher

"A flicker of recognition must pass through most teachers and parents when they read Horrid Henry. **There's a tiny bit of him in all of us.**" —Nancy Astee, *Child Education*

"**As a teacher…it's great to get a series of books my class loves.** They go mad for Horrid Henry." —A teacher

"**Henry is a beguiling hero who has entranced millions of reluctant readers.**" —*Herald*

"An absolutely fantastic series and surely a winner with all children. Long live Francesca Simon and her brilliant books! More, more please!"　　　—A parent

"**Laugh-out-loud reading for both adults and children alike.**" —A parent

"**Horrid Henry certainly lives up to his name, and his antics are everything you hope your own child will avoid—which is precisely why younger children so enjoy these tales.**"—*Independent on Sunday*

"Henry might be unbelievably naughty, totally wicked, and utterly horrid, but **he is frequently credited with converting the most reluctant readers into enthusiastic ones**…superb in its simplicity." —*Liverpool Echo*

"will make you laugh out loud."
—Sunday Times

"Parents reading them aloud may be consoled to discover that Henry can always be relied upon to behave worse than any of their own offspring." —*Independent*

"**What is brilliant about the books is that Henry never does anything that is subversive**. She creates an aura of supreme naughtiness (of which children are in awe) but points out that he operates within a safe and secure world...**eminently readable** books." —Emily Turner, *Angels and Urchins*

"Inventive and funny, with appeal for boys and girls alike, and super illustrations by Tony Ross." —Jewish Chronicle

"Accompanied by fantastic black-and-white drawings, the book is a joy to read. **Horrid Henry has an irresistible appeal to everyone—child and adult alike!** He is the child everyone is familiar with—irritating, annoying, but you still cannot help laughing when he gets into yet another scrape. Not quite a devil in disguise but you cannot help wondering at times! No wonder he is so popular!" — Angela Youngman

Horrid Henry by Francesca Simon

Horrid Henry

Horrid Henry Tricks the Tooth Fairy

Horrid Henry and the Mega-Mean Time Machine

Horrid Henry's Stinkbomb

Horrid Henry and the Mummy's Curse

Horrid Henry and the Soccer Fiend

HORRID HENRY

TRICKS THE TOOTH FAIRY

Francesca Simon

Illustrated by Tony Ross

visit us at www.abdopublishing.com

Reinforced library bound edition published in 2013 by Spotlight, a division of the ABDO Group, PO Box 398166, Minneapolis, MN 55439. Spotlight produces high-quality reinforced library bound editions for schools and libraries. Published by agreement with Sourcebooks, Inc.

Printed in the United States of America, North Mankato, Minnesota.
042012
092012

 This book contains at least 10% recycled materials.

Library of Congress Cataloging-in-Publication Data

This book was previously cataloged with the following information:
Simon, Francesca.
  Horrid Henry tricks the tooth fairy / Francesca Simon ; illustrated by Tony Ross.
     p. cm.
  [1. Behavior—Fiction. 2. Humorous stories] I. Ross, Tony, ill. II. Title.
  PZ7.S604Hrf 2009
  [Fic]—dc22
                        2008047822
ISBN 978-1-59961-191-4 (reinforced library edition)

All Spotlight books are reinforced library bindings and manufactured in the United States of America.

For Victor and Susan Bers,
and all our good times

CONTENTS

1 Horrid Henry Tricks the
   Tooth Fairy   1

2 Horrid Henry's Wedding   21

3 Moody Margaret Moves In   41

4 Horrid Henry's New Teacher   67

1

HORRID HENRY TRICKS THE TOOTH FAIRY

"It's not fair!" shrieked Horrid Henry. He trampled on Dad's new flower bed, squashing the pansies. "It's just not fair!"

Moody Margaret had lost two teeth. Sour Susan had lost three. Clever Clare lost two in one day. Rude Ralph had lost four, two top and two bottom, and could spit to the blackboard from his desk. Greedy Graham's teeth were pouring out.

Even Weepy William had lost one—and that was ages ago.

Every day someone swaggered into school showing off a big black toothy gap and waving fifty cents or even a dollar that the Tooth Fairy had brought. Everyone, that is, but Henry.

"It's not fair!" shouted Henry again. He yanked on his teeth. He pulled, he pushed, he tweaked, and he tugged.

They would not budge.

His teeth were superglued to his gums.

"Why me?" moaned Henry, stomping on the petunias. "Why am I the only one who hasn't lost a tooth?"

Horrid Henry sat in his fort and scowled. He was sick and tired of other kids flaunting their ugly wobbly teeth and disgusting holes in their gums. The next person who so much as mentioned the word "tooth" had better watch out.

"HENRY!" shouted a squeaky little voice. "Where are you?"

Horrid Henry hid behind the branches.

"I know you're in the fort, Henry," said Perfect Peter.

"Go away!" said Henry.

"Look, Henry," said Peter. "I've got something wonderful to show you."

Henry scowled. "What?"

"You have to see it," said Peter.

Peter never had anything good to show. His idea of something wonderful was a new stamp, or a book about plants, or a gold star from his teacher saying how perfect he'd been. Still...

Henry crawled out.

"This better be good," he said. "Or you're in big trouble."

Peter held out his fist and opened it.

There was something small and white in Peter's hand. It looked like...no, it couldn't be.

Henry stared at Peter. Peter smiled as

wide as he could. Henry's jaw dropped.
This was impossible. His eyes must be
playing tricks on him.

Henry blinked. Then he blinked again.

His eyes were not playing tricks.
Perfect Peter, his *younger* brother, had a
black gap at the bottom of his mouth
where a tooth had been.

Henry grabbed Peter. "You colored in
your tooth with black crayon, you fak-
er."

"Have not!" shrieked Peter. "It fell
out. See."

Peter proudly poked his finger through
the hole in his mouth.

4

It was true. Perfect Peter had lost a
tooth. Henry felt as if a fist had slammed
into his stomach.

"Told you," said Peter. He smiled
again at Henry.

Henry could not bear to look at Peter's
gappy teeth a second longer. This was the
worst thing that had ever happened to
him.

"I hate you!" shrieked Henry. He was
a volcano pouring hot molten lava onto
the puny human foolish enough to get in
his way.

"AAAAGGGGHHHH!" screeched Peter, dropping the tooth.

Henry grabbed it.

"OWWWW!" yelped Peter. "Give me back my tooth!"

"Stop being horrid, Henry!" shouted Mom.

Henry dangled the tooth in front of Peter.

"Nah nah ne nah nah," jeered Henry.

Peter burst into tears.

"Give me back my tooth!" screamed Peter.

Mom ran into the garden.

"Give Peter his tooth this minute," said Mom.

"No," said Henry.

Mom looked fierce. She held out her hand. "Give it to me right now."

Henry dropped the tooth on the ground.

"There," said Horrid Henry.

"That's it, Henry," said Mom. "No pudding tonight."

Henry was too miserable to care.

Peter scooped up his tooth. "Look, Mom," said Peter.

"My big boy!" said Mom, giving him a hug. "How wonderful."

"I'm going to use my money from the Tooth Fairy to buy some stamps for my collection," said Peter.

"What a good idea," said Mom.

Henry stuck out his tongue.

"Henry's sticking out his tongue at me," said Peter.

"Stop it, Henry," said Mom. "Peter, keep that tooth safe for the Tooth Fairy."

"I will," said Peter. He closed his fist tightly around the tooth.

7

★ ★ ★

Henry sat in his fort. If a tooth wouldn't fall out, he would have to help it. But what to do? He could take a hammer and smash one out. Or he could tie string around a tooth, tie the string around a door handle, and slam the door. Eek! Henry grabbed his jaw.

On second thought, perhaps not. Maybe there was a less painful way of losing a tooth. What was it the dentist always said? Eat too many sweets and your teeth will fall out?

Horrid Henry sneaked into the kitchen. He looked to the right. He looked to the left. No one was there. From the living room came the screechy scratchy sound of Peter practicing his cello.

Henry dashed to the cupboard where Mom kept the candy jar. Candy day was Saturday, and today was Thursday. Two whole days before he got into trouble.

Henry stuffed as many sticky candies into his mouth as fast as he could.

Chomp Chomp Chomp Chomp.

Chomp Chew Chomp Chew.

Chompa Chew Chompa Chew.

Chompa…Chompa…

Chompa…

Chompa…

Chew.

Henry's jaw started to slow down. He put the last sticky toffee in his mouth and forced his teeth to move up and down.

Henry started to feel sick. His teeth felt even sicker. He wiggled them hopefully. After all that sugar one was sure to fall out. He could see all the comics he would buy with his dollar already.

Henry wiggled his teeth again. And again.

Nothing moved.

Rats, thought Henry. His mouth hurt. His gums hurt. His tummy hurt. What did a boy have to do to get a tooth?

Then Henry had a wonderful, spectacular idea. It was so wonderful that he hugged himself. Why should Peter get a dollar from the Tooth Fairy? Henry would get that dollar, not him. And how? Simple. He would trick the Tooth Fairy.

The house was quiet. Henry tiptoed
into Peter's room. There was Peter,
sound
asleep, a big smile on his face. Henry
sneaked his hand under Peter's pillow and
stole the tooth.

Tee hee, thought Henry. He tiptoed
out of Peter's room and bumped into
Mom.

"AAAAGGGHH!" shrieked Henry.

"AAAAGGGHH!" shrieked Mom.

"You scared me," said Henry.

"What are you doing?" said Mom.

"Nothing," said Henry. "I thought I
heard a noise in Peter's room and went to
check."

Mom looked at Henry. Henry tried to
look sweet.

"Go back to bed, Henry," said Mom.

Henry scampered to his room and put
the tooth under his pillow. Phew. That
was a close call. Henry smiled. Wouldn't

11

that crybaby Peter be furious the next
morning when he found no tooth and no
money?

Henry woke up and felt under his pillow.
The tooth was gone. Hurray, thought
Henry. Now for the money.

Henry searched under the pillow.

Henry searched on top of the pillow. He
searched under the covers, under Teddy,
under the bed, everywhere. There was no
money.

Henry heard Peter's footsteps
pounding down the hall.

"Mom, Dad, look," said Peter. "A
whole dollar coin from the Tooth Fairy!"

"Great!" said Mom.

"Wonderful!" said Dad.

What?! thought Henry.

"Should I share it with you, Mom?" said Peter.

"Thank you, darling Peter, but no thanks," said Mom. "It's for you."

"I'll take it," said Henry. "There are tons of comics I want to buy. And some—'

"No," said Peter. "It's mine. Get your own tooth."

Henry stared at his brother. Peter would never have dared to speak to him like that before.

Horrid Henry pretended he was a pirate captain pushing a prisoner off the plank.

"OWWW!" shrieked Peter.

"Don't be horrid, Henry," said Dad.

Henry decided to change the subject fast.

"Mom," said Henry. "How does the Tooth Fairy *know* who's lost a tooth?"

"She looks under the pillow," said Mom.

"But how does she know whose pillow to look under?"

"She just does," said Mom. "By magic."

"But how?" said Henry.

"She sees the gap between your teeth," said Mom.

Aha, thought Henry. That's where he'd gone wrong.

That night Henry cut out a small piece of black paper, wet it, and covered his two bottom teeth. He smiled at himself in the mirror. Perfect, thought Henry. He smiled again.

Then Henry stuck a pair of dracula

teeth under his pillow. He tied a string around the biggest tooth, and tied the string to his finger. When the Tooth Fairy came, the string would pull on his finger and wake him up.

All right, Tooth Fairy, thought Henry. You think you're so smart. Find your way out of this one.

The next morning was Saturday. Henry woke up and felt under his pillow. The string was still attached to his finger, but the dracula teeth were gone. In their place was something small and round...

"My dollar coin!" crowed Henry. He grabbed it.

The dollar coin was plastic.

There must be some mistake, thought Henry. He checked under the pillow again. But all he found was a folded piece of bright blue paper, covered in stars.

Henry opened it. There, in tiny gold
letters, he read:

Nice try Henry
The Tooth Fairy

"Rats," said Henry.

From downstairs came the sound of
Mom shouting.

"Henry! Get down here this minute!"

"What now?" muttered Henry,
heaving his heavy bones out of bed.

"Yeah?" said Henry.

Mom held up an empty jar.

"Well?" said Mom.

Henry had forgotten all about the candy.

"It wasn't me," said Henry automatically. "We must have mice."

"No candy for a month," said Mom. "You'll eat apples instead. You can start right now."

Ugh. Apples. Henry hated all fruits and vegetables, but apples were the worst.

"Oh no," said Henry.

"Oh yes," said Mom. "Right now."

Henry took the apple and bit off the teeniest, tiniest piece he could.

CRUNCH. CRACK.

Henry choked. Then he swallowed, gasping and spluttering.

His mouth felt funny. Henry poked around with his tongue and felt a space.

He shoved his fingers in his mouth,
then ran to the mirror.

His tooth was gone.

He'd swallowed it.

"It's not fair!" shrieked Horrid Henry.

2

HORRID HENRY'S WEDDING

"I'm not wearing these horrible clothes and that's that!"

Horrid Henry glared at the mirror. A stranger smothered in a lilac ruffled shirt, green satin knickerbockers, tights, pink cummerbund tied in a floppy bow, and pointy white satin shoes with gold buckles glared back at him.

Henry had never seen anyone looking so silly in his life.

"Aha ha ha ha ha!" shrieked Horrid Henry, pointing at the mirror.

Then Henry peered more closely. The ridiculous looking boy was him.

Perfect Peter stood next to Horrid Henry. He too was smothered in a lilac ruffled shirt, green satin knickerbockers, tights, pink cummerbund, and pointy white shoes with gold buckles. But, unlike Henry, Peter was smiling.

"Aren't they adorable!" squealed Prissy Polly. "That's how my children are always going to dress."

Prissy Polly was Horrid Henry's horrible older cousin. Prissy Polly was always squeaking and squealing:

"Eeek, it's a speck of dust."

"Eeek, it's a puddle."

"Eeek, my hair is a mess."

But when Prissy Polly announced she was getting married to Pimply Paul and wanted Henry and Peter to be ring bearers, Mom said yes before Henry could stop her.

"What's a ring bearer?" asked Henry suspiciously.

"A ring bearer carries the wedding rings down the aisle on a satin cushion," said Mom.

"And throws confetti afterward," said Dad.

Henry liked the idea of throwing confetti. But carrying rings on a cushion? No thanks.

"I don't want to be a ring bearer," said Henry.

"I do, I do," said Peter.

"You're going to be a ring bearer, and that's that," said Mom.

"And you'll behave yourself," said Dad. "It's very kind of cousin Polly to ask you."

Henry scowled.

"Who'd want to be married to *her?*" said Henry. "I wouldn't if you paid me a million dollars."

But for some reason the groom, Pimply Paul, did want to marry Prissy Polly. And, as far as Henry knew, he had not been paid one million dollars.

Pimply Paul was also trying on his wedding clothes. He looked ridiculous in a black top hat, lilac shirt, and a black jacket covered in gold swirls.

"I won't wear these silly clothes," said Henry.

"Oh be quiet, you little brat," snapped Pimply Paul.

Horrid Henry glared at him.

"I won't," said Henry. "And that's final."

"Henry, stop being horrid," said Mom. She looked extremely silly in a big floppy hat dripping with flowers.

Suddenly Henry grabbed at the lace ruffles around his throat.

"I'm choking," he gasped. "I can't breathe."

24

Then Henry fell to the floor and rolled around.

"Uggggghhhhhhh," moaned Henry. "I'm dying."

"Get up this minute, Henry!" said Dad.

"Eeek, there's dirt on the floor!" shrieked Polly.

"Can't you control that child?" hissed Pimply Paul.

"I DON'T WANT TO BE A
RING BEARER!" howled Horrid
Henry.

"Thank you so much for asking me to
be a ring bearer, Polly," shouted Perfect
Peter, trying to be heard over Henry's
screams.

"You're welcome," shouted Polly.

"Stop that, Henry!" ordered Mom.
"I've never been so ashamed in my life."

"I hate children," muttered Pimply
Paul under his breath.

Horrid Henry stopped. Unfortunately,
his ring bearer clothes looked as fresh and
crisp as ever.

All right, thought Horrid Henry. You
want me at this wedding? You've got me.

Prissy Polly's wedding day arrived. Henry
was delighted to see rain pouring down.
How mad Polly would be.

Perfect Peter was already dressed.

"Isn't this going to be fun, Henry?" said Peter.

"No!" said Henry, sitting on the floor. "And I'm not going."

Mom and Dad stuffed Henry into his ring bearer clothes. It was hard, heavy work.

Finally everyone was in the car.

"We're going to be late!" shrieked Mom.

"We're going to be late!" shrieked Dad.

"We're going to be late!" shrieked Peter.

"Good!" muttered Henry.

Mom, Dad, Henry, and Peter arrived at the church. Boom! There was a clap of thunder. Rain poured down. All the other guests were already inside.

"Watch out for the puddle, boys," said Mom, as she leapt out of the car. She opened her umbrella.

Dad jumped over the puddle.

Peter jumped over the puddle.

Henry jumped over the puddle, and tripped.

SPLASH!

"Oopsy," said Henry.

His ruffles were torn, his knickerbockers were filthy, and his satin shoes were soaked.

Mom, Dad, and Peter were covered in muddy water.

Perfect Peter burst into tears.

"You've ruined my ring bearer clothes," sobbed Peter.

Mom wiped as much dirt as she could off Henry and Peter.

"It was an accident, Mom, really," said Henry.

"Hurry up, you're late!" shouted Pimply Paul.

Mom and Dad dashed into the church. Henry and Peter stayed outside, waiting to make their entrance.

Pimply Paul and his best man, Cross Colin, stared at Henry and Peter.

"You look like a mess," said Paul.

"It was an accident," said Henry.

Peter sniveled.

"Now be careful with the wedding rings," said Cross Colin. He handed

Henry and Peter a satin cushion each,
with a gold ring on top.

A great quivering clump of lace and
taffeta and bows and flowers approached.
Henry guessed Prissy Polly must be
lurking somewhere underneath.

"Eeek," squeaked the clump. "Why
did it have to rain on my wedding?"

"Eeek," squeaked the clump again.
"You're filthy."

Perfect Peter began to sob. The satin
cushion trembled in his hand. The ring
balanced precariously near the edge.

Cross Colin snatched Peter's cushion.

"You can't carry a ring with your hand
shaking like that," snapped Colin.
"You'd better carry them both, Henry."

"Come *on*," hissed Pimply Paul.
"We're late!"

Cross Colin and Pimply Paul dashed
into the church.

The music started. Henry pranced down the aisle after Polly. Everyone stood up.

Henry beamed and bowed and waved. He was King Henry the Horrible, smiling graciously at his cheering subjects before he chopped off their heads.

As he danced along, he stepped on Polly's long, trailing dress.

Riiiiip.

"Eeeeek!" squeaked Prissy Polly.

Part of Polly's train lay beneath Henry's muddy satin shoe.

That dress was too long anyway, thought Henry. He kicked the fabric out of the way and stomped down the aisle.

The bride, groom, best man, and ring bearers assembled in front of the minister.

Henry stood…and stood…and stood. The minister droned on…and

on…and on. Henry's arm holding up the cushion began to ache.

This is boring, thought Henry, jiggling the rings on the cushion.

Boing! Boing! Boing!

Oooh, thought Henry. I'm good at ring tossing.

The rings bounced.

The minister droned.

Henry was a famous pancake chef, tossing the pancakes higher and higher and higher…

Clink clunk.

The rings rolled down the aisle and vanished down a small grate.

Oops, thought Henry.

"May I have the rings, please?" said the minister.

Everyone looked at Henry.

"He's got them," said Henry desperately, pointing at Peter.

"I do not," sobbed Peter.

Henry reached into his pocket. He found two pieces of old chewing gum, some gravel, and his lucky pirate ring.

"Here, use this," he said.

At last, Pimply Paul and Prissy Polly were married.

Cross Colin handed Henry and Peter a basket of pink and yellow rose petals each.

"Throw the petals in front of the bride and groom as they walk back down the aisle," whispered Colin.

"I will," said Peter. He scattered the petals before Pimply Paul and Prissy Polly.

"So will I," said Henry. He hurled a handful of petals in Pimply Paul's face.

"Watch it, you little brat," snarled Paul.

"Windy, isn't it?" said Henry. He hurled another handful of petals at Polly.

"Eeek," squeaked Prissy Polly.

"Everyone outside for the photographs," said the photographer.

Horrid Henry loved having his picture taken. He dashed out.

"Pictures of the bride and groom first,"
said the photographer.

Henry jumped in front.

Click.

Henry peeked from the side.

Click.

Henry stuck out his tongue.
Click.
Henry made horrible rude faces.
Click.

"This way to the reception!" said
Cross Colin.

★ ★ ★

The wedding party was held in a nearby hotel.

The adults did nothing but talk and eat, talk and drink, talk and eat.

Perfect Peter sat at the table and ate his lunch.

Horrid Henry sat under the table and poked people's legs. He crawled around and squashed some toes. Then Henry got bored and drifted into the next room.

There was the wedding cake, standing alone, on a little table. It was the most beautiful, delicious looking cake Henry had ever seen. It had three layers and was covered in luscious white icing and yummy iced flowers and bells and leaves.

Henry's mouth watered.

I'll just taste a teeny weeny bit of petal, thought Henry. No harm in that.

He broke off a morsel and popped it in his mouth.

Mmmmm boy! That icing tasted great.

Perhaps just one more bite, thought Henry. If I take it from the back, no one will notice.

Henry carefully selected an icing rose from the bottom tier and stuffed it in his mouth. Wow.

Henry stood back from the cake. It looked a little uneven now, with that rose
missing from the bottom.

I'll just even it up, thought Henry. It was the work of a moment to break off a rose from the middle tier and another from the top.

Then a strange thing happened.

"Eat me," whispered the cake. "Go on."

Who was Henry to ignore such a request?

He picked out a few crumbs from the back.

Delicious, thought Henry. Then he took a few more. And a few more. Then he dug out a nice big chunk.

"What do you think you're doing?" shouted Pimply Paul.

Henry ran around the cake table. Paul ran after him.

Around and around and around the cake they ran.

"Just wait till I get my hands on you!" snarled Pimply Paul.

39

Henry dashed under the table.

Pimply Paul lunged for him and missed.

SPLAT.

Pimply Paul fell headfirst onto the cake.

Henry slipped away.

Prissy Polly ran into the room.

"Eeek," she shrieked.

"Wasn't that a lovely wedding?" sighed Mom on the way home. "Funny they didn't have a cake, though."

"Oh yes," said Dad.

"Oh yes," said Peter.

"OH YES!" said Henry. "I'll be glad to be a ring bearer anytime."

3

MOODY MARGARET
MOVES IN

Mom was on the phone.

"Of course we'd be delighted to have Margaret," she said. "It will be no trouble at all."

Henry stopped breaking the tails off Peter's plastic horses.

"WHAT?" he howled.

"Shh, Henry," said Mom. "No, no," she added. "Henry is delighted, too. See you Friday."

"What's going on?" said Henry.

"Margaret is coming to stay while her parents go on vacation," said Mom.

Henry was speechless with horror.

"She's going to stay...here?"

"Yes," said Mom.

"How long?" said Henry.

"Two weeks," said Mom brightly.

Horrid Henry could not stand Moody Margaret for more than two minutes.

"Two weeks?" he said. "I'll run away! I'll lock her out of the house, I'll pull her hair out, I'll..."

"Don't be horrid, Henry," said Mom. "Margaret's a lovely girl and I'm sure we'll have fun."

"No we won't," said Henry. "Not with that moody old grouch."

"I'll have fun," said Perfect Peter. "I love having guests."

"She's not sleeping in my room," said Horrid Henry. "She can sleep in the basement."

"No," said Mom. "You'll move into

Peter's room and let Margaret have your bed."

Horrid Henry opened his mouth to scream, but only a rasping sound came out. He was so appalled he could only gasp.

"Give…up…my…room!" he choked. "To…Margaret?"

Margaret spying on *his* treasures, sleeping in *his* bed, playing with *his* toys while he had to share a room with Peter…

"No!" howled Henry. He fell on the floor and screamed. "NO!!"

"I don't mind giving up my bed for a guest," said Perfect Peter. "It's the polite thing to do. Guests come first."

Henry stopped howling just long enough to kick Peter.

"Owww!" screamed Peter. He burst into tears, "Mom!"

"Henry!" yelled Mom. "You horrid boy! Say sorry to Peter."

"She's not coming!" shrieked Henry. "And that's final."

"Go to your room!" yelled Mom.

Moody Margaret arrived at Henry's house with her parents, four suitcases, seven boxes of toys, two pillows, and a trumpet.

"Margaret won't be any trouble," said her mom. "She's always polite, eats everything, and never complains. Isn't that right, Precious?"

"Yes," said Margaret.

"Margaret's no fusspot," said her dad. "She's good as gold, aren't you, Precious?"

"Yes," said Margaret.

"Have a lovely vacation," said Mom.

"We will," said Margaret's parents.

The door slammed behind them.

45

Moody Margaret marched into the living room and swept a finger across the mantel.

"It's not very clean, is it?" she said. "You'd never find so much dust at *my* house."

"Oh," said Dad.

"A little dust never hurt anyone," said Mom.

"I'm allergic," said Margaret. "One whiff of dust and I start to...sn...sn... ACHOOO!" she sneezed.

"We'll clean up right away," said Mom.

Dad mopped.
Mom swept.
Peter dusted.
Henry vacuumed.
Margaret directed.

46

"Henry, you've missed a big dust ball right there," said Margaret, pointing under the sofa.

Horrid Henry vacuumed as far away from the dust as possible.

"Not there, here!" said Margaret.

Henry aimed the vacuum at Margaret. He was a fire-breathing dragon burning his prey to a crisp.

"Help!" shrieked Margaret.

47

"Henry!" said Dad.

"Don't be horrid," said Mom.

"I think Henry should be punished," said Margaret. "I think he should be locked in his bedroom for three weeks."

"I don't have a bedroom to be locked up in 'cause you're in it," said Henry. He glared at Margaret.

Margaret glared back.

"I'm the guest, Henry, so you'd better be polite," hissed Margaret.

"Of course he'll be polite," said Mom. "Don't worry, Margaret. Any trouble, you come straight to me."

"Thank you," said Moody Margaret, smiling. "I will. I'm hungry," she added. "Why isn't supper ready?"

"It will be soon," said Dad.

"But I *always* eat at six o'clock," said Margaret, "I want to eat NOW."

"All right," said Dad.

Horrid Henry and Moody Margaret dashed for the seat facing the garden. Margaret got there first. Henry shoved her off. Then Margaret shoved him off.

Thud. Henry landed on the floor.

"Ouch," said Henry.

"Let the guest have the chair," said Dad.

"But that's *my* chair," said Henry. "That's where I *always* sit."

"Have my chair, Margaret," said Perfect Peter. "I don't mind."

"I want to sit here," said Moody Margaret. "I'm the guest so I decide."

Horrid Henry dragged himself around the table and sat next to Peter.

"OUCH!" shrieked Margaret. "Henry kicked me!"

"No I didn't," said Henry, outraged.

"Stop it, Henry," said Mom. "That's no way to treat a guest."

Henry stuck out his tongue at
Margaret. Moody Margaret stuck out her
tongue even further, then stomped on his
foot.

"OUCH!" shrieked Henry. "Margaret
kicked me!"

Moody Margaret gasped. "Oh I'm ever

so sorry, Henry," she said sweetly. "It was an accident. Silly me. I didn't mean to, really I didn't."

Dad brought the food to the table.

"What's *that?*" asked Margaret.

"Baked beans, corn on the cob, and chicken," said Dad.

"I don't like baked beans," said Margaret. "And I like my corn *off* the cob."

Mom scraped the corn off the cob.

"No, put the corn on a separate plate!" shrieked Margaret. "I don't like vegetables touching my meat."

Dad got out the pirate plate, the duck plate, and the "Happy birthday, Peter" plate.

"I want the pirate plate," said Margaret, snatching it.

"I want the pirate plate," said Henry, snatching it back.

"I don't mind which plate I get," said Perfect Peter. "A plate's a plate."

"No it isn't!" shouted Henry.

"I'm the guest," shouted Margaret. "I get to choose."

"Give her the pirate plate, Henry," said Dad.

"It's not fair," said Henry, glaring at his plate decorated with little ducks.

"She's the guest," said Mom.

"So?" said Henry. Wasn't there an ancient Greek who stretched all his guests on an iron bed if they were too short or lopped off their heads and feet if they were too long? That guy sure knew how to deal with horrible guests like Moody Margaret.

"Yuck," said Margaret, spitting out a mouthful of chicken. "You put salt on it!"

"Only a little," said Dad.

"I never eat salt," said Moody Margaret. "It's not good for me. And I always have peas at *my* house."

"We'll get some tomorrow," said Mom.

★ ★ ★

Peter lay asleep in the top bunk. Horrid
Henry sat listening by the door. He'd
scattered crumbs all over Margaret's bed.
He couldn't wait to hear her scream.

But there wasn't a sound coming from
Henry's room, where Margaret the
Invader lay. Henry couldn't understand it.

Sadly, he climbed into (oh, the shame
of it) the *bottom* bunk. Then he
screamed.
His bed was filled with jam, crumbs, and
something squishy squashy and horrible.

"Go to sleep, Henry!" shouted Dad.

That Margaret! He'd booby trap the
room, cut up her doll's clothes, paint her
face purple…Henry smiled grimly. Oh
yes, he'd show Moody Margaret.

Mom and Dad sat in the living room
watching TV.

Moody Margaret appeared on the
stairs.

"I can't sleep with that noise," she said.

Mom and Dad looked at each other.

"We are watching very quietly, dear," said Mom.

"But I can't sleep if there's any noise in the house," said Margaret. "I have very sensitive ears."

Mom turned off the TV and picked up her knitting needles.

Click click click.

Margaret reappeared.

"I can't sleep with that clicking noise," she said.

"All right," said Mom. She sighed a little.

"And it's cold in my bedroom," said Moody Margaret.

Mom turned up the heat.

Margaret reappeared.

"Now it's too hot," said Moody Margaret.

Dad turned down the heat.

"My room smells funny," said Margaret.

"My bed is too hard," said Margaret.

"My room is too stuffy," said Margaret.

"My room is too light," said Margaret.

"Good night, Margaret," said Mom.

"How many more days is she staying?" said Dad.

Mom looked at the calendar.

"Only thirteen," said Mom.

Dad hid his face in his hands.

"I don't know if I can live that long," said Dad.

TOOTA TOOT. Mom blasted out of bed.

TOOTA TOOT. Dad blasted out of bed.

TOOTA TOOT. TOOTA TOOT.

TOOTA TOOT TOOT TOOT. Henry and Peter blasted out of bed.

Margaret marched down the hall, playing her trumpet.

TOOTA TOOT. TOOTA TOOT.

TOOTA TOOT TOOT TOOT
TOOT.

"Margaret, would you mind playing
your trumpet a little later?" said Dad,
clutching his ears. "It's six o'clock in the
morning."

"That's when I wake up," said
Margaret.

"Could you play a little more softly?"
said Mom.

"But I have to practice," said Moody
Margaret.

The trumpet blared through the house.
TOOT TOOT TOOT.

Horrid Henry turned on his radio.
BOOM BOOM BOOM.

Margaret played her trumpet louder.
TOOT! TOOT! TOOT!

Henry blasted his radio as loud as
he could.

BOOM! BOOM! BOOM!

"Henry!" shrieked Mom.

"Turn that down!" bellowed Dad.

"Quiet!" screamed Margaret. "I can't practice with all this noise." She put down her trumpet. "And I'm hungry. Where's my breakfast?"

"We have breakfast at eight," said Mom.

"But I want breakfast now," said Margaret.

Mom had had enough.

"No," said Mom firmly. "We eat at eight."

Margaret opened her mouth and screamed. No one could scream as long, or as loud, as Moody Margaret.

Her piercing screams echoed through the house.

"All right," said Mom. She knew when she was beaten. "We'll eat now."

★ ★ ★

Henry's diary.

Monday I put crumbs in Margaret's bed. She put jam, crusts, and slugs in mine.

Tuesday Margaret found my secret cookies and chips and ate every single one.

Wednesday I can't play cd's at night because it disturbs grumpy-face Margaret.

Thursday I can't sing because it disturbs frog-face.

Friday I can't breathe because it disturbs misery-guts.

Saturday I can stand it No Longer

That night, when everyone was asleep, Horrid Henry crept into the living room and picked up the phone.

"I'd like to leave a message," he whispered.

Bang bang bang bang bang.

Ding dong! Ding dong! Ding dong!

Henry sat up in bed.

Someone was banging on the front door and ringing the bell.

"Who could that be at this time of night?" yawned Mom.

Dad peeked through the window then opened the door.

"Where's my baby?" shouted Margaret's mom.

"Where's my baby?" shouted Margaret's dad.

"Upstairs," said Mom. "Where else?"

"What's happened to her?" shrieked Margaret's mom.

"We got here as quick as we could!" shrieked Margaret's dad.

Mom and Dad looked at each other. What was going on?

"She's fine," said Mom.

Margaret's mom and dad looked at each other. What was going on?

"But the message said it was an emergency and to come at once," said Margaret's mom.

"We cut short our vacation," said Margaret's dad.

"What message?" said Mom.

"What's going on? I can't sleep with all this noise," said Moody Margaret.

Margaret and her parents had gone home.

"What a terrible mix-up," said Mom.

"Such a shame they cut short their vacation," said Dad.

"Still…" said Mom. She looked at Dad.

"Hmmm," said Dad.

"You don't think that Henry…" said Mom.

"Not even Henry could do something so horrid," said Dad.

Mom frowned.

"Henry!" said Mom.

Henry continued sticking Peter's stamps together.

"Yeah?"

"Do you know anything about a message?"

"Me?" said Henry.

"You," said Mom.

"No," said Henry. "It's a mystery."

"That's a lie, Henry," said Perfect Peter.

"Is not," said Henry.

"Is too," said Peter. "I heard you on the phone."

Henry lunged at Peter. He was a mad bull charging the matador.

"YOWWWWW," shrieked Peter.

Henry stopped. He was in for it now. No allowance for a year. No candy for ten years. No TV ever.

Henry squared his shoulders and waited for his punishment.

Dad put his feet up.

"That was a terrible thing to do," said Dad.

Mom turned on the TV.

"Go to your room," said Mom.

Henry bounced upstairs. Your room. Sweeter words were never spoken.

4

HORRID HENRY'S NEW TEACHER

"Now Henry," said Dad. "Today is the first day of school. A chance for a fresh start with a new teacher."

"Yeah, yeah," scowled Horrid Henry.

He hated the first day of school. Another year, another teacher to show who was boss. His first teacher, Miss Marvel, had run screaming from the classroom after two weeks. His next teacher, Mrs. Zip, had run screaming from the classroom after one day. Breaking in new teachers wasn't easy, thought Henry, but someone had to do it.

Dad got out a piece of paper and waved it.

"Henry, I never want to read another report card like this again," he said. "Why can't your report cards be like Peter's?"

Henry started whistling.

"Pay attention, Henry," shouted Dad. "This is important. Look at this report card."

HENRY'S REPORT CARD

It has been horrible Teaching Henry this year. He is rude, lazy, and disruptive. The worst student I have ever taught.

Behavior: Horrid

English: Horrid

Math: Horrid

Science: Horrid

P.E.: Horrid

"What about *my* report card?" said
Perfect Peter.

Dad beamed.

"Your report card was perfect, Peter,"
said Dad. "Keep up the wonderful work."

PETER'S REPORT CARD

It has been a pleasure
teaching Peter this year. He is
polite, hardworking, and
cooperative. The best student I
Behavior: have ever taught.

English: Perfect

Math: Perfect

Science: Perfect

P.E.: Perfect

Peter smiled proudly.

"You'll just have to try harder,
Henry," said Peter, smirking.

Horrid Henry was a shark sinking his teeth into a drowning sailor.

"OWWWW," shrieked Peter. "Henry bit me!"

"Don't be horrid, Henry!" shouted Dad. "Or no TV for a week."

"I don't care," muttered Henry. When he became king he'd make it a law that parents, not children, had to go to school.

Horrid Henry pushed and shoved his way into class and grabbed the seat next to Rude Ralph.

"Nah nah ne nah nah, I've got a new football," said Ralph.

Henry didn't have a football. He'd kicked his through Moody Margaret's window.

"Who cares?" said Horrid Henry.

The classroom door slammed. It was Mr. Nerdon, the toughest, meanest, nastiest teacher in the school.

"SILENCE!" he said, glaring at them with his bulging eyes. "I don't want to hear a sound. I don't even want to hear anyone breathe."

The class held its breath.

"GOOD!" he growled. "I'm Mr. Nerdon."

Henry snorted. What a stupid name.

"Nerd," he whispered to Ralph.

Rude Ralph giggled.

"Nerdy Nerd," whispered Horrid Henry, snickering.

Mr. Nerdon walked up to Henry and jabbed his finger in his face.

"Quiet, you horrible boy!" said Mr. Nerdon. "I've got my eye on you. Oh yes. I've heard about your other teachers. Bah! I'm made of stronger stuff. There will be no nonsense in *my* class."

We'll see about that, thought Henry.

"Our first math problems for the year are on the board. Now get to work," ordered Mr. Nerdon.

Horrid Henry had an idea.

Quickly he scribbled a note to Ralph.

Ralph — I bet you that I can make Mr. Nerdon run screaming out of class by the end of lunchtime.

No way, Henry

If I do will you give me your new football?

O.K. But if you don't, you have to give me a dollar.

O.K.

Horrid Henry took a deep breath and went to work. He rolled up some paper, stuffed it in his mouth, and spat it out. The spitball whizzed through the air and pinged Mr. Nerdon on the back of his neck.

Mr. Nerdon wheeled round.

"You!" snapped Mr. Nerdon. "Don't you mess with me!"

"It wasn't *me!*" said Henry. "It was Ralph."

"Liar!" said Mr. Nerdon. "Sit at the back of the class."

Horrid Henry moved his seat next to Clever Clare.

"Move over, Henry!" hissed Clare. "You're on my side of the desk."

Henry shoved her.

"Move over yourself," he hissed back.

Then Horrid Henry reached over and broke Clare's pencil.

"Henry broke my pencil!" shrieked Clare.

Mr. Nerdon moved Henry next to Weepy William.

Henry pinched him.

Mr. Nerdon moved Henry next to Tough Toby.

Henry jiggled the desk.

Mr. Nerdon moved Henry next to Lazy Linda.

Henry scribbled all over her paper.

Mr. Nerdon moved Henry next to Moody Margaret.

Moody Margaret drew a line down the middle of the desk.

"Cross that line, Henry, and you're dead," said Margaret under her breath.

Henry looked up. Mr. Nerdon was writing spelling words on the board.

Henry started to erase Margaret's line.

"Stop it, Henry," said Mr. Nerdon, without turning round.

Henry stopped.

Mr. Nerdon continued writing.

Henry pulled Margaret's hair.

Mr. Nerdon moved Henry next to Beefy Bert, the biggest boy in the class.

Beefy Bert was chewing his pencil and trying to add 2 + 2 without much luck.

Horrid Henry inched his chair onto Beefy Bert's side of the desk.

Bert ignored him.

Henry poked him.

Bert ignored him.

Henry hit him.

POW!

The next thing Henry knew he was lying on the floor, looking up at the ceiling. Beefy Bert continued chewing his pencil.

"What happened, Bert?" said Mr. Nerdon.

"I dunno," said Beefy Bert.

"Get up off the floor, Henry!" said Mr. Nerdon. A faint smile appeared on the teacher's slimy lips.

"He hit me!" said Henry. He'd never felt such a punch in his life.

"It was an accident," said Mr. Nerdon. He smirked. "You'll sit next to Bert from now on."

That's it, thought Henry. Now it's war.

"How absurd, to be a nerdy bird," said Horrid Henry behind Mr. Nerdon's back.

Slowly Mr. Nerdon turned and walked toward him. His hand was clenched into a fist.

"Since you're so good at rhyming," said Mr. Nerdon. "Everyone write a poem. Now."

Henry slumped in his seat and groaned. A poem! Yuck! He hated poems. Even the word *poem* made him want to throw up.

Horrid Henry caught Rude Ralph's eye. Ralph was grinning and mouthing,

"A dollar, a dollar!" at him. Time was running out. Despite Henry's best efforts, Mr. Nerdon still hadn't run screaming from the class. Henry would have to act fast to get that football.

What horrible poem could he write? Horrid Henry smiled. Quickly he picked up his pencil and went to work.

"Now, who's my first victim?" said Mr. Nerdon. He looked around the room. "Susan! Read your poem."

Sour Susan stood up and read:

> "Bow wow
> Bow wow
> Woof woof woof
> I'm a dog, not a cat, so...
> SCAT!"

"Not enough rhymes," said Mr.
Nerdon. "Next..." He looked round
the room. "Graham!"

Greedy Graham stood up and read:

"Chocolate chocolate chocolate sweet,
Cakes and doughnuts can't be beat.
Ice cream is my favorite treat
With lots and lots of pie to eat!"

"Too many rhymes," said Mr. Nerdon.
"Next..." He scowled at the class.
Henry tried to look as if he didn't want
the teacher to call on him.

"Henry!" snapped Mr. Nerdon. "Read
your poem!"

Horrid Henry stood up and read:

"Pirates puke on stormy seas,
Giants spew on top of trees."

Henry peeked at Mr. Nerdon. He
looked pale. Henry continued to read:

"Kings are sick in golden bowls,
Dogs throw up on Dad's casseroles."

Henry peeked again at Mr. Nerdon. He
looked green. Any minute now, thought
Henry, and he'll be out of here
screaming. He read on:

"Babies love to make a mess,
Down the front of Mom's best dress.

And what car ride would be complete,
Without the stink of last night's treat?"

"That's enough," choked Mr. Nerdon.

"Wait, I haven't got to the good part," said Horrid Henry.

"I said that's enough!" gasped Mr. Nerdon. "You fail."

He made a big black mark in his book.

"I threw up on the boat!" shouted Greedy Graham.

"I threw up on the plane!" shouted Sour Susan.

"I threw up in the car!" shouted Dizzy Dave.

"I said that's enough!" ordered Mr. Nerdon. He glared at Horrid Henry. "Get out of here, all of you! It's lunchtime."

Rats, thought Henry. Mr. Nerdon was one tough teacher.

Rude Ralph grabbed him.

"Ha ha, Henry," said Ralph. "You lose. Gimme that dollar."

"No," said Henry. "I've got until the end of lunch."

"You can't do anything to him between now and then," said Ralph.

"Oh yeah?" said Henry. "Just watch me."

Then Henry had a wonderful, spectacular idea. This was it. The best plan he'd ever had. Someday someone would stick a plaque on the school wall celebrating Henry's genius. There would be songs written about him. He'd probably even get a medal. But first things first. In order for his plan to work to perfection, he needed Peter.

Perfect Peter was playing hopscotch with his friends Tidy Ted and Spotless Sam.

"Hey Peter," said Henry. "How would you like to be a real member of the Purple Hand?"

The Purple Hand was Horrid Henry's secret club. Peter had wanted to join for ages, but naturally Henry would never let him.

Peter's jaw dropped open.

"Me?" said Peter.

"Yes," said Henry. "If you can pass the secret club test."

"What do I have to do?" said Peter eagerly.

"It's tricky," said Henry. "And probably much too hard for you."

"Tell me, tell me," said Peter.

"All you have to do is lie down right there below that window and stay absolutely still. You can't move until I tell you to."

"Why?" said Peter.

"Because that's the test," said Henry.

Perfect Peter thought for a moment.

"Are you going to drop something on me?"

"No," said Henry.

"OK," said Peter. He lay down obediently.

"And I need your shoes," said Henry.

"Why?" said Peter.

Henry scowled.

"Do you want to be in the secret club or not?" said Henry.

"I do," said Peter.

"Then give me your shoes and be quiet," said Henry. "I'll be checking on you. If I see you moving one little bit, you can't be in my club."

Peter gave Henry his sneakers, then lay still as a statue.

Horrid Henry grabbed the shoes, then dashed up the stairs to his classroom.

It was empty. Good.

Horrid Henry went over to the window and opened it. Then he stood there, holding one of Peter's shoes in each hand.

Henry waited until he heard Mr. Nerdon's footsteps. Then he went into action.

"Help!" shouted Horrid Henry. "Help!"

Mr. Nerdon entered. He saw Henry and glowered.

"What are you doing here? Get out!"

"Help!" shouted Henry. "I can't hold on to him much longer…he's slipping… aaahhh, he's fallen!"

Horrid Henry held up the empty shoes.

"He's gone," whispered Henry. He peeked out of the window. "Ugghh, I can't look."

Mr. Nerdon went pale. He ran to the window and saw Perfect Peter lying still and shoeless on the ground below.

"Oh no," gasped Mr. Nerdon.

"I'm sorry," panted Henry. "I tried to hold on to him, honest, I—"

"Help!" screamed Mr. Nerdon. He raced down the stairs. "Police! Fire! Ambulance! Help! Help!"

He ran over to Peter and knelt by his still body.

"Can I get up now, Henry?" said Perfect Peter.

"What!?" gasped Mr. Nerdon. "What did you say?"

Then the terrible truth dawned. He, Ninius Nerdon, had been tricked.

"YOU HORRID BOY! GO STRAIGHT TO THE PRINCIPAL— NOW!" screeched Mr. Nerdon.

Perfect Peter jumped to his feet.

"But...but—" spluttered Perfect Peter.

"Now!" screamed Mr. Nerdon. "How dare you! To the principal!"

"AAAGGGHHHH," shrieked Peter.

He slunk off to the principal's office, weeping.

Mr. Nerdon turned to race up the stairs to grab Henry.

"I'll get you, Henry!" he screamed. His face was white. He looked as if he were going to faint.

"Help," squeaked Mr. Nerdon.

Then he fainted.

Clunk! Thunk! Thud!

NEE NAW NEE NAW NEE NAW.

When the ambulance arrived, the only person lying on the ground was Mr. Nerdon. They scooped him onto a stretcher and took him away.

The perfect end to a perfect day, thought Horrid Henry, throwing his new football in the air. Peter sent home in disgrace. Mr. Nerdon gone for good. Even the news that scary Miss Battle-Axe would be teaching Henry's class didn't bother him. After all, tomorrow was another day.

And now for a sneak peek at one of the laugh–out–loud stories in *Horrid Henry and the Mega-Mean Time Machine*

PERFECT PETER'S REVENGE

Perfect Peter had had enough. Why oh why did he always fall for Henry's tricks?

Every time it happened he swore Henry would never ever trick him again. And every time he fell for it. How *could* he have believed that there were fairies at the bottom of the garden? Or that there was such a thing as a Fangmangler? But the time machine was the worst. The very very worst. Everyone had teased him. Even Goody-Goody Gordon asked him if he'd seen any spaceships recently.

Well, never again. His mean, horrible brother had tricked him for the very last time.

I'll get my revenge, thought Perfect Peter, pasting the last of his animal stamps into his album. I'll make Henry sorry for being so mean to me.

But what horrid mean nasty thing could he do? Peter had never tried to take revenge on anyone.

He asked Tidy Ted.

"Mess up his room," said Ted.

But Henry's room was already a mess.

He asked Spotless Sam.

"Put a spaghetti stain on his shirt," said Sam.

But Henry's shirts were already stained.

Peter picked up a copy of his favorite magazine *Best Boy*. Maybe it would have some handy hints on the perfect revenge. He searched the table of contents:

- IS YOUR BEDROOM AS TIDY AS IT COULD BE?
- TEN TOP TIPS FOR PLEASING YOUR PARENTS
- HOW TO POLISH YOUR TROPHIES

- WHY MAKING YOUR BED IS GOOD FOR YOU
- READERS TELL US ABOUT THEIR FAVORITE CHORES!

Reluctantly, Peter closed *Best Boy* magazine. Somehow he didn't think he'd find the answer inside. He was on his own.

I'll tell Mom that Henry eats candy in his bedroom, thought Peter. Then Henry would get into trouble. Big big trouble.

But Henry got into trouble all the time. That wouldn't be anything special.

I know, thought Peter, I'll hide Mr. Kill. Henry would never admit it, but he couldn't sleep without Mr. Kill. But so what if Henry couldn't sleep? He'd just come and jump on Peter's head or sneak downstairs and watch scary movies.

I have to think of something really, really horrid, thought Peter. It was hard for Peter to think horrid thoughts, but Peter was determined to try.

He would call Henry a horrid name, like Ugly Toad or Poo Poo Face. *That* would show him.

But if I did, Henry would hit me, thought Peter.

Wait, he could tell everyone at school that Henry wore diapers. Henry the big diaper. Henry the big smelly diaper. Henry diaper face. Henry poopy pants. Peter smiled happily. That would be the perfect revenge.

Then he stopped smiling. Sadly, no one at school would believe that Henry still wore diapers. Worse, they might think that Peter still did! Eeeek.

I've got it, thought Peter, I'll put a muddy twig in Henry's bed. Peter had read a great story about a younger brother who'd done just that to a mean older one. That would serve Henry right.

But was a muddy twig enough revenge for all of Henry's crimes against him?

No it was not.

I give up, thought Peter, sighing. It was hopeless. He just couldn't think of anything horrid enough.

Peter sat down on his beautifully made bed and opened *Best Boy* magazine.

TELL MOM HOW MUCH YOU LOVE HER!

shrieked the headline.

And then a dreadful thought tiptoed

into his head. It was so dreadful, and so horrid, that Perfect Peter could not believe that he had thought it.

"No," he gasped. "I couldn't." That was too evil.

But...but...wasn't that exactly what he wanted? A horrid revenge on a horrid brother?

"Don't do it!" begged his angel.

"Do it!" urged his devil, thrilled to get the chance to speak. "Go on, Peter! Henry deserves it."

YES! thought Peter. He would do it. He would have revenge!

Perfect Peter sat down at the computer. Tap tap tap.

Dear Margaret,
I love you. Will you marry me?

Peter printed out the note and carefully scrawled:

HENry

There! thought Peter proudly. That looks just like Henry's writing. He folded the note, then sneaked into the garden, climbed over the wall, and left it on the table inside Moody Margaret's Secret Club tent.

We cannot believe Peter would be so awful to try to trick his wonderful brother Henry. You will not believe what happens next even if we tell you. Perfect Peter is not very perfect in Horrid Henry's next hilarious book: *Horrid Henry and the Mega-Mean Time Machine*.

HORRID HENRY

Henry is dragged to dancing class against his will; vies with Moody Margaret to make the yuckiest Glop; goes camping; and tries to be good like Perfect Peter—but not for long.

HORRID HENRY and THE MEGA-MEAN TIME MACHINE

Horrid Henry reluctantly goes for a hike; builds a time machine and convinces Perfect Peter that boys wear dresses in the future; Perfect Peter plays one of the worst tricks ever on his brother; and Henry's aunt takes the family to a fancy restaurant, so his parents bribe him to behave.

HORRID HENRY'S STINKBOMB

Horrid Henry uses a stinkbomb as a toxic weapon in his long-running war with Moody Margaret; uses all his tricks to win the school reading competition; goes for a sleepover and retreats in horror when he finds that other people's houses aren't always as nice as his own; and has the joy of seeing Miss Battle-Axe in hot water with the principal when he knows it was all his fault.

About the Author

Photo: Francesco Guidicini

Francesca Simon spent her childhood on the beach in California and then went to Yale and Oxford Universities to study medieval history and literature. She now lives in London with her family. She has written over forty-five books and won the Children's Book of the Year in 2008 at the Galaxy British Book Awards for *Horrid Henry and the Abominable Snowman*.